Originally published as Sammie in de zomer in Belgium
and Holland by Clavis Uitgeverij, Hasselt—Amsterdam, 2018
English translation from the Dutch by Clavis Publishing Inc., New York

Visit us on the Web at www.clavis-publishing.com.

Sammy in the Summer written and illustrated by Anita Bijsterbosch

ISBN 978-1-60537-433-8

This book was printed in January 2019 at Wai Man Book Binding (China) Ltd.
Flat A, 9/F., Phase 1, Kwun Tong Industrial Centre, 472-484 Kwun Tong Road,
Kwun Tong, Kowloon, H.K.

First Edition
10 9 8 7 6 5 4 3 2 1

Clavis Publishing supports the First Amendment and celebrates the right to read.

SAMMY
in the Summer

Anita Bijsterbosch

Clavis
NEW YORK

It's summer. Sammy and his little horse Hob love to play outside. Today they are splashing in the swimming pool. Sammy sprays water in the air with the garden hose. "It's raining!" he says.

Sammy hops on his bike.
Hob is in front, in the little basket.
It's a short ride to the beach.
"Look, Hob," Sammy says,
"we are almost there!"

Time to put on some sunscreen.
"Here, Hob—you also get
sunscreen on your snout.
Now we won't get a sunburn."

Sammy fills his red bucket with wet sand.
He turns the bucket upside down.
What do you think Sammy is making?

Sammy and Hob are heading home.
Ding! Ding! They hear a bell.
It's the sound of an ice cream truck!
Sammy buys a cone.

Yum, this ice cream is delicious!
"Would you like to taste too, Hob?"
Sammy asks.

Sammy and Hob stop at the garden.
Sammy planted seeds in the spring.
The plants have really grown!

Sammy picks tomatoes,
cucumbers, lettuce, and a melon.
He puts them in a basket.
Hey, where did Hob go?

Now there is time to fly a kite.
Look how high it goes.
Sammy and Hob play
until the sun sets.
Summer is so much fun!

Hob is waiting for Sammy
at the table. Sammy and Hob
enjoy a picnic under the umbrella.
Sammy eats a piece of melon.
The fruit is sweet and juicy.

Sammy built a sandcastle!
He even made a moat to go around it.
Hob is having fun playing in the castle.

Sammy gets out of the pool
and dries himself off with
a towel. "Let's go to the beach,
Hob!" he says.